They're Watching
Volume III

Ukiyoto Publishing

All global publishing rights are held by

Ukiyoto Publishing
Published in 2022

Content Copyright © Ukiyoto

ISBN 9789362694553

*All rights reserved.
No part of this publication may be reproduced, transmitted, or stored in a retrieval system, in any form by any means, electronic, mechanical, photocopying, recording or otherwise, without the prior permission of the publisher.*

The moral rights of the authors have been asserted.

This is a work of fiction. Names, characters, businesses, places, events, locales, and incidents are either the products of the author's imagination or used in a fictitious manner. Any resemblance to actual persons, living or dead, or actual events is purely coincidental.

This book is sold subject to the condition that it shall not by way of trade or otherwise, be lent, resold, hired out or otherwise circulated, without the publisher's prior consent, in any form of binding or cover other than that in which it is published.

"For thin is the veil betwixt man and the godless deep. The skies are haunted by that which it was madness to know; and strange abominations pass evermore between earth and moon and athwart the galaxies. Unnamable things have come to us in alien horror and will come again. And the evil of the stars is not as the evil of earth."

— *Clark Ashton Smith, The Beast Of Averoigne*

Contents

Short Story by Abinaya. K	1
Short Story by Samantha Lucas	6
Short Story by Farzana Habib	15
Poem by Adanu Michaels	23
Short Stories by Plabi Pradhan	27
About the Authors	45

Short Story by Abinaya. K

A Girl in the Philippines

I have never seen a ghost in my life, when I was young I grew up with ghost stories, cartoons and movies. I was too naive to believe everything as if it's true. I believed that supernatural elements have control over humans, because the ghosts also were humans once, but when I came to know that ghost is a lie, I was taken aback felt like it's a betrayal, I thought why people want to scare everyone, though I am aware that ghost is a lie, the innate creeps refused to subside from my life, since fear plays vulnerable role in everyone's life. As I grew up, I encountered innumerable creeps, which were horrendous and more horrible than ghosts, then I learned that insecurities and injustices which are created by humans haunted my life. Ghosts are not malicious and perilous but humans' evil actions are a threat for survival. As I was depressed in the dark pitch night, I suddenly stumbled upon a book on my table titled " Ghost too had dreams " I have no idea, who kept that book on my table, I began to start reading the book, as I began to read, I heard the voice which explained the lines from the book, I am freaked out but I remained less daunted because I learned that human's evil actions are scarier than ghosts. I asked, " What are you up to?" I said, the world is unfair to my dreams and desires. I further said that, even if you are going to kill me, I am least bothered because at least then I could find answers by interrogating God, why are humans not how they are supposed to be? I never thought that I would see a ghost in my life and I would bear out my pains to the ghost. It was like the cartoon that I watched when I was young, I never thought that I would speak to the ghost which chilled my spine when I was young. When I narrated all my angst, I saw the tears in ghost eyes and it began to speak by telling that, " this is what life gives to humans and this is how the world will look when you are depressed". The ghost said that, you can't blame the world for its unfairness, that is not how God created the world. Since the world is infested with humans, whose life is filled with sins, it will always intimidate the innocent desires and dreams. The ghost held my hands and it said that, " you should never attend the death call until you live in this world with greatest satisfaction". The ghost told me, don't say that you are ready to die to confront God, just because you can't achieve your dreams, God has already given all the required answers even before you confront, all the answers will be visible only if you fight for your dreams, all the answers will found in your legacies thus go after your dreams, the ghost further said, "you can change anything, no matter how unfair it is". The ghost firmly ingrained an unshakeable determination in my depressed mind, and it suddenly became quiet, I could barely get my head around, what brought the ghost to my place? I asked the ghost, why did you die? did you achieve your dreams? Is there any legacy of you? The moment I interrogated it, its eyes flooded with tears and it said, I too had dreams but I left the world with uncultivated dreams and without experiencing the greatest satisfaction of living, I asked, would you mind to bear out your heart to me? Ghost replied that, it holds one of reasons for my presence and the ghost began to narrate by telling,

Iam Lee Guen - young from South Korea, who had dreams and aspirations. I had a dream of becoming a Singer, by carrying those dreams in my heart, I moved to the Philippines after I completed my high school. I joined the Philippines University of Music. Initially I felt like a fish out of water, it took time for me to socialize with other people, I saw a lot of people who came from various countries. I struggled very hard to fit in because it's a new country, I made friends in my University, we began to wander in the streets of the Philippines, I learned more about their cultures and festivals but I still missed my country. I began to work hard to study music to become a K Pop Idol, I slated various plans to work on my album to make my debut as soon as I graduate from the University, many Philippines friends also helped me out with their innovative ideas to make my music more appealing, everyone in the world had American Dream, but I hankered for Asian Dream to obtain American Dream. I thought I must cultivate my talents in Asian countries, where it emerged to reach America. Philippines became my second home, it embraced me as if I belong there, Philippines never splurged any distaste towards me, but my life snatched away because of unfairness, I encountered hostile people there who said that I can't achieve my dreams and it's a pipe dream and I died when my album was rejected because of those people 's vengeance. They said they are native people and I'm just a girl with Asian Dreams, and the ghost became silent. I cried after I heard the ghost's story and the ghost rooted for me to fight the battle and not to die before the defeat. " It turned out well", the director said and the producer said, "It's a wrap" and the Korean actress Park Shin-who played the role ghost and Philippines actress Isabel Granada who played the role narrator gave interview to the press, "Everyone must watch our film to comprehend the significance of respecting Asians and how the life turns dark due to splurging hatred among Asians, Dreams belong to everyone whether its Asian Dream or American Dream", and the movie "A Girl in Philippines" was released and it amassed more than 3 million views in film industry.

Short Story by Samantha Lucas

Following Joy

I lost my best friend when I was twenty-one. We had just finished university by then, and we had a bright future ahead of us. Well, I was the only one left with a bright future between the two of us.

My name is Georgina, but you can call me George. I am now thirty-four. I have a successful e-commerce marketing role, and I sell organic toiletries on my website. I have a partner who works in real estate, and my family is doing well. I have everything I need at present to say that I am already a mad woman. But I still look back often to my late best friend Joy's death thirteen years ago.

Joy and I met when I just moved to Saint Agnes School in Quezon City. I was a transferee in our junior year, as my family has just relocated to Manila from Pampanga. I was initially the subject of teasing by my classmates as I was taller than them. I got my height from my mother, who used to be a ramp model in decades past. Joy saw that I was struggling, and she immediately made me feel welcome by lending me her copy of our Science textbook. Since I was a new student, some of my textbooks have not yet arrived. I felt touched by her gesture, and this helped me ease my way not just into our lessons, but in the social dynamics as well of our batch.

Joy was popular in our all-girls school not just because she was one of its honor students, but also because she had a sunny personality. She took me under her wing, and made me tag along with her at the school paper. Not only did I instantly have a club, but I also had a packed schedule ahead of me, thanks to the people I had to interview for our features section. Joy helped me pass our group projects by including me in the groups that she was part of. She let me sit with her group of girlfriends every lunch and recess. In no time, I was able to seamlessly blend in with the crowd. I was doing well not just academically, but socially as well. All thanks to Joy.

Things were smooth sailing most of the time. I was no longer teased for being the tall new student. I received acceptance and respect from most of the students.

One day, Joy and I were having snacks while studying at her house when she made me promise not to tell anyone else about the revelation that she was about to divulge. Of course, I immediately complied. Joy leaned and whispered into my ear: "I can see the future sometimes, and I know that I will die young." I got furious at her because I was not in the mood for pranks. She assured me that she was not kidding. She supported her statement by telling me that she could foresee when our teachers will give pop quizzes, so she would study for lessons that were not yet discussed in class. She knew that her father will pass away before her seventh birthday in a plane crash, so she asked her mother if she can remain in Manila instead of joining her estranged father to a trip to his provincial hometown. She also predicted that her mother will be scammed by one of her business partners, so she warned her mother to pull out her investments before it was too late. She was not able to stop her father from making that ill-fated trip, so she unflinchingly told her mother to get out of that business fast. She sadly told me though, that there is no way for her to cheat her way out of her own death. She knows that it will be in a vehicular accident, but she cannot see the specifics. I asked her why she cannot stop her own death and why she is even letting me know all of this. She told me that while she cannot see right through me, nor can she predict my future, she knows for a fact that my life will not be easy due to circumstances beyond my control. She warned me to establish a career first before learning how to drive. She told me that by confiding with me, she feels lighter because she is not alone with her secret.

I asked her how I should go on with my life with the burden of her confession on my shoulders. She asked me to just carry on, because life is too short. She asked me to study hard and do my best in high school, college, and work. Lastly, she asked me to be open to dating and having a stable partner so that I will not be alone. While I was puzzled, I just said yes. We continued with our studying after that.

I followed my friend Joy's advice. I finished high school in the Top Ten of our batch, along with Joy. She chose to study Philosophy at a university known for its pre-law and law programs. I entered a business school where I pursued Creative Writing.

University life was challenging because I was not as wealthy or privileged as my wealthy blockmates. My school was known for having elite students due to its expensive tuition fees, which explains why my blockmates had expensive cars and fancy clothes. I became a wallflower, since I did not party with them or eat at the restaurants that they frequented. I ended up becoming a consistent Dean's Lister, and I was able to focus on my academics. My Creative Writing track enabled me to hone my skills in storytelling, while taking units in business to give myself an edge among other future creatives. My internship at a lifestyle website gave me a macro view of the workforce and the creative industry that I wanted to join. I was later absorbed once I graduated with honors, and a university service award for excellence in student volunteerism.

Meanwhile, Joy excelled not just as a consistent Dean's Lister, but also as a community developer. She worked with her university's organization that focused on teaching nearby public high school student's life skills to help them have a better mindset. We regularly met up on weekends, and I was very proud of her work with her students. She was featured in the newspaper a few times for her work with these students, and later on, her internship at a renowned NGO earned her a leadership excellence award at her university. She also became Summa cum Laude, and was able to deliver a moving speech about living as if each day was her last on her graduation day.

We never spoke about her revelation about seeing the future again. However, I was brutally reminded of her gift when Joy passed away in a car accident at the age of twenty-one. She was driving her car in a highway, and she was rushing home to make it in time for her shift at the NGO that hired her after graduation. Sadly, a truck swerved and flattened her car in the process. In just a split second, I lost my best friend and closest ally.

I mourned her death, then eventually returned to work and my everyday routine. I was writing an article on a slow day when I just started talking to Joy. I was all alone in the office, because my coworkers were all having *merienda* during that time. I just said "Joy, I'm scared. I know that I should be comfortable by now because I have a stable job, a healthy relationship, and a steady paycheck. But Joy, I am scared." I just stared blankly into space when I distinctly heard Joy say, "you should resign and join the startup that emailed you." I was stunned. I immediately thought that I was just imagining things, but I wanted to probe further if it *really* was Joy. I answered, "but Joy, I am leaving a fat paycheck to join a local company that has not proved anything yet. Can you imagine, they are thinking of purely operating *online*? I mean, is there a decent company that 100% operates through an online store?" Joy then laughed and said "just resign and join that company. E-commerce is the future. Save yourself NOW!" I then had a quick vision of Joy standing in front of me in her university uniform with a stern look on her face. She was furious when she said that I should save myself. It was both startling and terrifying. Before I knew it, she was gone, and I was all alone in the office again.

My coworkers returned an hour later and we exchanged gossip and small talk. Before shutting down my company laptop, I emailed my confirmation to the e-commerce venture's interview invitation. I left the office and went straight home to think.

Joy passed away before even knowing what e-commerce is. For her to say that must mean that she is seeing something bad. I was having a few issues with my boss, who was excluding me from some important meetings. I then typed my resignation letter. By the time I printed and signed it, I knew that I should trust Joy and her gift.

I tendered my resignation the next day. While my boss was surprised, she approved my request for immediate resignation and she told me that I do not have to serve my thirty day notice. I left the office without even saying goodbye to most of my coworkers, and by five p.m. of that same day, I was already hired by the e-commerce venture.

It turns out that my former boss and a few of my coworkers were involved in a scandal with a shady foreign offshoring venture. They were raided and investigated a few weeks later, and the scandal was reported by both local and international press. If I had stayed with them, I would have been part of the investigation, which was something that I did not need. I immediately visited Joy's grave to thank her.

My life by then was not easy because I had to adjust to a new environment in the e-commerce venture. We had a slow start, and it took a few years before our company experienced the tremendous growth that was promised to us by our angel investors and IT developers. My partner Franz and I were also doing well. He was excelling as a real estate broker, as he balanced his job with his post-graduate studies. I later invested in my own business, which was an organic personal goods line distribution. I sold them on my website, and my business grew as well. My bosses later absorbed my business into the company, and the purchase allowed me to buy a new condo and self-publish the book that I wrote. I wanted to impart knowledge to the youth, so I wrote a book on business, online growth, and trusting my own gut. I dedicated my book to Joy.

I wonder how Joy would react to my new book. It was her dream to write one when she was still alive. I guess I do not have to use my imagine anymore because I still believe that she is always with me, one way or another. I think she is proud of me. And I hope that she knows that I am proud to be her friend, for as long as I shall live.

I have yet to see and hear Joy again. I hope that she is already in a better place, and that she knows that my life is beautiful thanks to all help. I am hoping that she still watches over me. For now, I will continue to work hard and hopefully, I can write another book. Perhaps my next one will be about the unbreakable power of friendship.

Short Story by Farzana Habib

Dead Ringer

As Janey's coffin was lowered onto the ground Adam Graham looked away. The funeral had a been a small affair, twenty-five people showed up. An 8 year relationship was now over and buried into the ground, along with his dreams. No, their dreams to move forward. There would never be a white wedding in the Himalayas now or a house made from wood and glass in front of the beach. Adam did not want to talk to anyone so he decided to excuse himself and search for his car. He just hated funerals.

Adam picked up the pace. Once he got in, he began to search for a small flask filled with something called "fireball" a warm orangish liquid that burned the throat. Adam took a few quick sips to steady himself and put the metal flask back into the glovebox. After what seemed like a long time his mom knocked on the window to be let in. She took off the black feathered mess that sat on top of her head, buckled up and was ready to go home. Flora lived in Veudreuil-Dorian. A suburban in greater Montreal. It was home to approximately 38,000 people and was a great place to raise a family. It was a small looking house that had three bedrooms, 2 baths and a newly renovated basement complete with sound-proofing walls, and a bar. Flora got out of the car and quickly started for the steps of her house. After fetching a brassy looking key underneath a false rock, the old woman walked inside.

She shed out her clothes and locked herself inside the bathroom. Water and wine always made her feel better. Her son opted for the same thing except he hid another flask, this time full of Jack Daniels. No one felt like cooking that night so Adam dialed for pizza along with other fried favorites, in an attempt to eat away at his sadness. It did not help very much but he went to bed around 1 am while his mom stayed back. Flora sneakily logged onto Adams navy blue HP laptop and surfed the net for a bit. Tonight she was not looking through her emails or shopping for planters Flora was going to make multiple profiles of her son on various dating sites like Ok Cupid, eHarmony and maybe even Tinder. She could not find too many that suited her but his had to be done. She uploaded a recent picture of Adam, one taken during her 55th birthday party. She had typed out the following onto his profile "A scorpion 38 year author looking for friendship romance and fun in a woman who loves to go out long walks, eat Thai food, read religiously and save the world one day at a time."

It was 4:42 AM and something went "ding" multiple times in his room. Adam sat up in bed and reached for his Iphone.

" What the—" Multiple requests were coming in from Ok Cupid, Tinder and something called the Escape

Adam rubbed his eyes and dismissed everything. He was not ready to date! not even the women his mother approved of.

"Good morning Mom, is there anything you want to tell me?" Flora had her back to him and was busy frying something on the stove. The kitchen smelled like fresh batter, fruits and coffee.

Adam got straight the point. " I do not want to date any time soon Ma, I am going to take this time to work on my latest manuscript and see where that takes me, so don't bother introducing me to any of your friends daughters or nieces.

Flora sighed and piled his plate with food. He ate in a hurry because he wanted some peace and quiet. He was going to drive to the nearest Starbucks and spend the remainder of his day there.

Adam walked out of the house and towards the car. He was about open the car door, when a 5'4 amber haired, doe eyed woman blocked the way.

He had no time for this but she looked like she had all the time in the world.

"Hi are you Adam Graham?"

"Yes I am and I have no—"

I am Nicole and I noticed your profile on Escape this morning. I was hoping that we could talk or go out for coffee"

"Get in" Adam gestured towards his car.

Nicole squealed and talked non-stop till they got to Starbucks.

Nicole was 29. They had gone to the same high school. She completed university in Toronto in Psychology, masters as well and was now working as counselor for people who suffer from eating disorders, addictions and sexual trauma. She ordered the drinks and he found the perfect table but something told him he was not going to get much writing done today. She was very talkative and made him laugh. Over the course of the next few hours, well until closing time. Nicole and Adam talked about everything. There was just something about her that put him to ease, she was very insightful and pretty too… Adam got to know that she was into water sports, loved to travel like he did, had fostered a kitten and wrote in her spare time.

There must have been something in the coffee because Adam let Nicole know about Janey. She didn't say anything but left him, her number. It was 10pm when they departed. Adam was feeling better and he had agreed to meet Nicole again the next morning.

Flora was nowhere to be seen the next morning, she left a note saying that she was busy with a friend and hoped that Nicole was worth his time. His mom had done research on the girl after she pried every detail out of him last night.

Nicole decided to see him that morning. She wore no makeup and had on a lilac colored dress. Janey loved lilacs. They had brunch at "Allo mon Coco" Adam settled for crab cakes benedict and she happily munched her way through a tower of apple and cheddar pancakes. Janey loved the combination of apples and cheddar too. after brunch Nicole and Adam spent the next few hours at a flea market looking at bits and pieces of practically everything.

Adam went straight to the booth that sold movies and books and Nicole was skimming through romance novels and necklaces. At the end, Adam bought all the DVDs to underworld and she a necklace made from black pearls.

Adam paid for the necklace and dropped her home.

Nicole and Adam had become a couple at this point and they spent as much time as possible. Date night now happened 3 times a week and she was slowly helping him overcome his grief. Adam believed that he will always love Janey, but it felt nice to have her presence around. Nicole in return hoped that he really and truly liked her. She never liked Janey very much but she was determined to become a better woman then dead Jamey. Nicole paid attention whenever he spoke very fondly of his wife with that look in his eyes and took notes on what she was like.

Nobody liked it when she was herself, but maybe Adam will like it if she was more like Janey.

After 6 months of dating Nicole texted Adam to meet her at Le Colbert, An Italian restaurant. He did not ask any questions. Life was great, his mom finally stopped pestering him, she approved of her and his book was really coming along. It was about two lovers who died a tragic death but meet again in the afterlife. He dedicated it to Janey.

Adam got there at 8:00 and she walked in at 8:05. Adam did not know what to say. Nicole had changed into somebody else. She dyed her auburn hair black, wore grey contacts, had on a leather dress that brought attention to her assets and walked around in a pair of black platforms. Nicole looked exactly like Jamey when he first brought her here six years ago. He was suddenly feeling very nervous but she looked confident as hell. She kissed him on the lips and opened the bottle of wine. She had already ordered "Surf N Turf" for him

She filled up his glass with Sauvignon Blanc and then hers, repeatedly.

"Do you like it Adam?" Nicole asked

"I have liked you for so long but I couldn't tell you that night, you brought Janey in here and I served you that evening. You were going to ask her to marry you and all I could do was just watch." So I left Montreal that same night and decided to only come back after I've made something of myself" I've lost all that weight, people notice me now and I know you like me too" This was how it was meant to be ...

Adam gulped down the wine in seconds and felt very dizzy, he was suddenly experiencing chest pains and his heart was racing

"Are you alright darling?"

Her voice sounded very distant and then everything went still.

# Poem by Adanu Michaels

My Ocean is Watching

Where must I take my search?

I have wandered every city

Counting Town to Town

Surveyed Village to Village

Learning every "Hi, Hello and Hey"

But not an atom of smile have I found

I wandered in vain

Through the Forests too, I have journeyed

Encountered the "Evil, bad and ugly"

Studied wild Animals and dwelt with them

Dined and wined with Kings and Queens of the Jungle

Raced with the fastest creatures of the forest

But no, the smile I seek is not there to behold

I journeyed in vain

I accepted an invitation from the Desert

I sacrificed "Shelter, Health and Wealth for the Desert"

I felt every dryness of the world

I was in company of the strangest beings in the Universe

But that smile was nowhere to be found

I sacrificed in vain

Then came, the Mountain calling

I climbed with joy to a Mountain even taller than the Everest

There, I could see the beauty of the whole world

And how Mother Earth suffers in "Pain, Immorality and Injustice"

My only Companion was the Cloud

But that smile seem too far away

I climbed in vain

The ocean came whispering

Tip-toeing through my dried heart

Floating in Love, Peace and Joy

In the mildest of voice she says to me

"You can be the Wave and I, the Ocean"

Then I said to her

"Don't you ever leave me because I am dying to love you"

With a smile so bright, she says with full excitement

"You won't ever have to worry because I will be there like the Air you Breath

I am the Ocean of Smile."

Short Stories by Plabi Pradhan

Birthday Boy

Ritam pushed the door and it was completely dark inside the room. Suddenly some electric candles came on at once and

"Surprise!" Shweta shouted and greeted her fiancé "Happy Birthday".

In the gloomy light, they embraced each other.

"Hmm…so I have to warm you up Mr. Birthday Boy!" Shweta tickled Ritam and laughed out.

"Actually, it's so cold outside and that's why my body is a little cold," Ritam said hurriedly.

It was Ritam's birthday. His fiancée Shweta had planned everything for a perfect date night. The room was completely decorated, delicious foods were ready at the table, and a well-decorated bed for the duo, for they wanted to make love the whole night.

Shweta was about to turn the light on and Ritam pulled her towards himself by her waist and stumbled upon the bed. He was kissing all over her body. Shweta was trying to say "let's eat our supper first" but a numbness caught all over her body. She was thoroughly enjoying Ritam's love all over herself. He was a little more aggressive, a little more excited that night.

Finally, two lovers broke down on the bed tiredly after an hour of love-making. They were lying side by side holding their hands.

Outside the Moon was struggling with the dark, fast-moving clouds, which at once was leaving it clear and bright and the next moment was sweeping over it and again it was patchy dark.

One time when the moon was shining clearly, the moonlit spread all over their naked body, and with a lot of admiration Shweta kissed Ritam's forehead. She had felt a coldness by her lips and Ritam's face had seemed to her very whitish and pale. Just the moment she tried to see his face again, dark clouds again occupied the Moon and there was dark again.

Suddenly the doorbell rang and Shweta hurled at once and murmured "in this time! Who can be?"

She dressed up quickly and opened the door.

"Akash…! It's you! Now? What happened?" Shweta astonished.

"What happened to me? What happened to you damn! Why you were not picking up the bloody phone?" Akash cried out.

"But trust me I hadn't received any call, I swear. Okay ask Ritam, he is…"

Shweta's sentence was not completed, Akash said with amazement, "Ritam…! How can I ask him? What are you saying? I… I… am coming to give you the news."

"News? What news?" Shweta asked curiously.

"Ritam faced a fatal accident in the afternoon and just an hour ago he had died in the hospital. I was calling you continuously after admitting him to the hospital. But you hadn't picked up the call." Akash said within a breath.

"What the hell are you saying?" Shweta slapped over his face and said, "don't do this type of silly joke with me. Come, come inside. He is sleeping on my bed. We are together from the last one hour."

Akash was thinking how it can be, for he was at the hospital with Ritam from the afternoon and he had come to Shweta after seeing Ritam's dead body.

After going inside Shweta turned the light on and saw there was no one. She searched everywhere in the room, kitchen, bathroom but there was no sign of Ritam.

Are You Traveling Alone?

"One ticket… to Madhyamgram" I was gasping heavily.

"Oh … thank God I have got the train"!

I got on the ladies compartment and it was completely vacant. I was very happy to see the vacant compartment.

"Oh…I can remove my mask at least until anyone comes" I thought in my mind.

I had to go 1:30hrs by train to reach my M.Ed. college which was at Madhyamgram, Kolkata.

I was enjoying the clickety-clack sound of the train, the sound of horn and whistles. I was thoroughly enjoying the side scenic beauty also. There in the train, a continuous cassette was playing awakening about Covid. Yes, it was reasonable though, but the endless playing was annoying me.

The train crossed a few stations but except for some hawkers no passenger got into the train.

Though it was noon, but I started feeling a bit uneasy. I didn't know why! To ignore the bizarre feeling I started reading a book named "Winner stands alone" by Paulo Coelho.

Paulo Coelho is one of my favorite authors whom I love to read. But that time I didn't even concentrate on the book. I stood up and glanced all over the compartment, none was there.

"What has happened today? No one is getting into the compartment! Maybe due to the restrictions of Omicron!" I thought in my mind.

I was feeling an uneasiness, my sixth sense was alarming me something that I didn't know.

And just then I heard a coughing sound.

"Oh…so at least one person is here" I murmured.

I stood up again and saw a lady poorly dressed at the last of that compartment coughing frantically.

"Drink some water and wear a mask. Don't you know corona is increasing?" I said in a suggesting tone.

She was coughing and was not paying any attention to me. That seemed a little bit offensive to me for some time, though I immediately withdrew my thought and went to her with a bottle of water and offered to her politely. She took the bottle and drank water.

When she was drinking water I was thoroughly examining her. Her eyes were awkwardly white as if she had anemia. Her skin was brown. It seemed like she was a poor lady more likely a beggar.

"Please take this mask and wear it" I offered her a mask.

"I don't need it…we the poor don't need it." She talked for the first time.

"What? What kind of thought is this? Who told you corona will not catch poor?" I said with a little bit angry voice and ordered her "take the mask and wear it now".

She had taken it unwilling and when her hand touched mine, it was icing cold. I sheered a bit and said, "please wear some warm cloth". She started saying, "there was my house at the bank of the Icchamati river… because of the cyclone 'Amphan' I lost everything…my house…my clothes, my husband and my elder son too. No one came to help me… I lost everything… everything".

I was feeling pain to her, my heart was aching. With a choking voice, I said, "I can feel your pain, but what can you do now! Let it go and do a new start."

I went back to my seat where my bag was, to bring some money to give her. I took a 500rs note from my bag and as soon as I turned back I heard a scream, as if just right after me. I was startled. I peeped outside from the train's door. None was there, she was not there. "Do I just hear a scream? Where she has gone just now? Even the train didn't stop, no platform had come!" I said on my own. I was puzzled. I was searching her every corner of the compartment and I heard some new words in a new tone somewhat the same as the lady, I was talking to. From the microphone that was continuously announcing Covid rules alerting people to wear masks etc. that woman's voice was coming, saying that "Please save my younger son, he is taking his last breath, save him, save him…" And that tone was playing in a loop. I don't know how long time it was repeating the words. I was feeling very obnoxious and I started searching for something or someone I don't know in every corner of the compartment and at last, I saw a teenage boy wearing only a half pant staring at me steadily and giving me an erratic smile.

The next day I found myself in a railway hospital and from the staff I came to know that I was found unconscious from a train compartment. They were asking me formal questions but I skipped all and asked straightly "where is the boy? Where is the lady?" Everyone was surprised there. A person said, "But you had found alone there, do you have any other with you?" Now it was my turn to be surprised. I told them all that was happened and everyone's face was dead white and after a lot of requests I came to know that some months before a poor widow lady suffering from corona attempted suicide by jumping from a train's ladies compartment. She was suffering from Covid. Her villagers had driven her and her son as they both were Covid positive. They were homeless, foodless, without treatment, and failing to bear the pain may be the lady attempted suicide and died. After some days her son was also found dead in the same train compartment. His cause of death was corona. They also said that I was the third person with whom that incident had happened in the train compartment. I was wobbled upon hearing all this. I was traumatized. It had taken several months to be normal again.

Now each time I get into the train, my mind keeps spectating each co-traveler, who knows who is dead and who is alive, sitting among us!

Roommate

It was a usual day during the lockdown. I just finished my so-called "work from home" and it was a shit boring lecture cum meeting with the boss. "Shit man! This lockdown and this zoom call…oh… My headache! I must take a coffee".

I went to the kitchen for a cup of coffee.

"Those days were awesome… We had so much fun after office… Why..? Why this happened dear!"

Suddenly I heard the sound of the opening and then closing of the main door.

And just then… "Hey roomie, I'm home… bring a cup of coffee for me also."

At once I said "oh yes…sure. Wait… I'm coming…"

A current flowed all over my body. "What? What have I said just now!"

"Who told me to bring coffee!"

"No, it cannot happen…"

A stream of sweat was then flowing down from my spine.

My roommate, Sweata, died almost two months ago due to covid. How could she come back!!

That Locked Room

Dr. Samya Roy was a young, handsome professor of English literature. Recently he had joined the college. Prof. Samya was a devoted reader and a dedicated teacher. Nothing but reading and teaching were his favorite.

"This college's library is so big, haha... good for me", Samya mumbled.

"Sir, Principal sir is calling you, will you please...", Ramu asked. Ramu Das is one of the non-teaching staffs of this college. "Yeah, I'm going", said Prof. Samya.

Covid cases were growing day by day in India. Lockdown was declared in many areas. There was a notification to close all the education sectors. Prof. Samya became a little bit sad. It was just a few weeks of his joining, and suddenly this notification.

"How could I spend my days without teaching, without students", Prof. Samya sighed.

Days were going like a home prisoner. Everyone was disturbed, frustrated. But after some days Prof. Samya got some happiness in his life. Online classes were going to start. This news made him so happy because he always loved to teach.

After two months…

Prof. Samya went to college to check the exam paper. That day other few professors had also come to college to do the same task.

Prof. Samya was sitting in an empty classroom and checking students' answer papers.

"Sir…sir…can I ask you something?" A female voice said.

"Yes, you can", Prof. Samya replied without looking at her.

"Can you please explain to me the first para of 'Paradise Lost'?" She said.

Then Prof. Samya lifted his head and said, "of course, but didn't you attend the online classes? And what are you doing here in college? Students are not allowed here now. Why you have come to the college in such a situation of the pandemic?"

"Covid-19 can't do anything to me, sir…" she replied smilingly.

"Silly girl, don't take it so casually. Anyway, sit here I will explain to you "Paradise Lost".

Prof. Samya started explaining. One hour passed of their discussion. Prof. Samya said, "alright, now go to your home and study well. It's a wonderful classic. I hope you understand everything".

"Yes sir", she replied.

"Oh… what's your name, dear?" Prof. Samya asked.

"Sunayani… Sunayani Das..sir", she replied.

"Okay, wonderful name, now go back to your home," he said.

Sunayani left the room.

"Sir, do you need anything?" Ramu asked.

"Oh…Ramu da, yes. I am just thinking to go to you for a cup of coffee. I will take a break, from one hour I was giving lectures", Prof, Samya said.

"Sir, pardon me, but to whom you were giving lectures? You were checking answer sheets, are you okay?", Ramu asked.

"Certainly, I'm fine. Sunayani, a first-year student, had come and requested me to explain a chapter. Why? Didn't you see her at the gate, when she was coming in, or going out?" Asked Prof. Samya.

"Sunayani… Sunayani…" Ramu started babbling for a while. "But sir, are you sure, it was Sunayani?" Ramu asked with confusion.

"She told her name that. Why, what's the big deal?" Prof. Samya said annoyingly.

"Can you remember her face?" Ramu asked anxiously.

"Why can't I? She was here for almost one hour in front of me, but why are you saying this! Oh…Ramu da, please bring my coffee, my head is aching now." Prof. Samya said disturbingly.

"Sir please come here with me, I've something to show you, please come," Ramu said.

"Oh, Ramu da, now what? Aren't you going to give me a coffee?" Prof. Samya was feeling disturbed. "I have to check a lot of exam papers, I have to return to my home, and this Ramu da….uff…" He mumbled for a while.

"Okay let's go," said Prof. Samya.

They went to the end of the college building, there was a room.

Ramu opened the lock and said, "come with me, sir".

They entered into a room. It was an empty room, there was only a cupboard, a bed and nothing else. A ceiling fan was there also. Ramu opened the cupboard and brought a picture and said, "Sir, are you talking about this girl?"

"Yes, what are doing in the picture with her? And you are also very young in this picture! Though the girl is looking the same age, as I saw her a few hours ago. But it seems like an old picture." Prof. Samya said confusingly.

"Sunayani is my daughter sir," Ramu said.

"What, but why are you young in this photo, and sunayani is the same? Prof. Samya exclaimed.

"This photo is 20years old sir". Ramu said with an eerie smile.

"But...but the girl is now 20years old may be, as I saw her." Prof. Samya started babbling and started feeling uneasy.

He was willing to go out of the room, but he couldn't. It seemed like his feet were frozen.

Ramu started by saying... "Sunayani was a brilliant student, she loved to read so much. She was pursuing the first year of her English Hons. I was the gateman of this college. We were so happy in our life. One day I found Sunayani hanging from the ceiling fan in this room. Look, in that way, look, sir...look", Ramu pointed out to the ceiling fan.

Prof. Samya stared at the ceiling and saw Sunayani was hanging from the fan. Her eyes were open, she was smiling brutally. Her hairs were on her face.

Prof. Samya screamed in fear. He was also seeing that Ramu's face was changing, his eyes were coming out, and then…

Prof. Samya fainted.

The next day a non-teaching staff discovered Prof. Samya lying in front of that locked room.

After Prof. Samya got his sense his colleagues asked him about what was he doing there in front of that locked room. Also said that he was lying unconsciously there from yesterday.

Prof. Samya was not in the condition of replying. He said, "Ramu da, where is he? Sunayani?"

"Ramu da!" "Sunayani!" Some professors exclaimed. "How do you know him, you just joined a few months ago! And he died almost ten years ago. Some senior professors knew him. His daughter Sunayani was found dead in that room almost fifteen years ago, from where you were found. But why did you go there Samya?" They asked.

Prof. Samya was in complete shock. He started babbling alone "Was that real, yesterday's incidents, but they are saying Ramu da had died before, but why I was seeing him from my joining day? He always gave me coffee, brought papers… how could he then! Did I see a dream? These few months… everything was dreams… no… it can't be…."

They admitted Prof. Samya to a hospital. Perhaps they will never get to know what happened to Dr. Samya Roy that day.

About the Authors

Abinaya. K

Abinaya. K is an award winning poet and writer. She is an author of the book Courage To Fly High (Collection of 40 poems) Her poems were shortlisted for Dr. Anamika Poetry for GenZ Poets. She is currently pursuing I M A English in Holy Cross College. She has co-authored twelve anthologies. She has published her poetry in several reputed literary journals including Teenager Today, Storizen Magazine, I Quote Magazine, Inskpire, India Quartely and in Mt.Kenya Times Newspaper, South Africa.

Samantha Lucas

Samantha Gail B. Lucas has been blogging on her website, www.speakoutsam.com, since May 2017. She has since attended several conferences, workshops, and networking opportunities through her website. She regularly shares her favorite local finds, foodie adventures, charitable advocacies, and media partnerships. She graduated with an AB Humanities degree from the University of Asia and the Pacific. Her first book, *Speak Blog Live*, was published in October 2021, while her second book, *Speak Write Live*, was published in December 2021. Her first international book, *I Helped Myself,* was released in March 2022. She currently resides in Quezon City, Philippines.

Farzana Habib

Farzana Habib is a college student pursuing Social Sciences. She hopes to one day write children's books and plays. She loves all things food, traveling, watching movies, sketching, yoga and hiking. She has presently published 2 novels, 2 poetry collections and has participated in multiple anthologies. She is now currently working on a new novel titled *The Woman in the Painting*.

Adanu Michaels

Adanu Michaels is a Young African Poet and short story writer who writes across several themes with much reference to African culture. He is the author of *Trumpet of Rhapsody* and has contributed to several anthologies published by Ukiyoto Publishing. He is an Idoma son born to the Family of Mr. And Mrs Adanu James of Adoka district, Otukpo local government area of Benue state Nigeria.

Plabi Pradhan

Plabi Pradhan, is an Indian author of *Whenever A Poet's Heart Pops Up*. She has co-authored several anthologies. She was selected as one of the 100 writers in the #versesoflove writing contest, in February 2021 by Notion Press, and her poetry was published in their official anthology. She was selected among the Top 9 writers in the Bullet Tales contest in August 2021 and was selected among Top20 writers of India by Half Baked Beans Publishing in the Annual Micro-Fiction Competition 2021 and her micro-fictions had been published in their anthology. She was Awarded as "Literary Captain" in July 2021 and was nominated for the Author of the Year 2021 Award by StoryMirror Publication.

www.ingramcontent.com/pod-product-compliance
Lightning Source LLC
LaVergne TN
LVHW041555070526
838199LV00046B/1976